This edition first published in MMXX by Book House

Distributed by Black Rabbit Books
P.O. Box 3263
Mankato, Minnesota 56002

© MMXX The Salariya Book Company Ltd
All rights reserved.
No part of this book may be reproduced, stored in a retrieval system or transmitted in any form or by any means, electronic, mechanical, photocopying, recording or otherwise, without the written permission of the copyright owner

Cataloging-in-Publication Data is available from the Library of Congress

Printed in the United States
At Corporate Graphics,
North Mankato, Minnesota

9 8 7 6 5 4 3 2 1

ISBN: 978-1-912904-27-3

Additional illustrations:
Betty Branch, David Stewart, Max Marlborough, Margot Channing, and Shutterstock.

Consultant: Dr. Olivia Langmead is a marine conservation scientist. She holds research positions at the University of Plymouth, England, and the Marine Biological Association of the UK. Her work is at the marine science/policy interface, specifically the interactions between people and the marine environment. Her interests include seabed habitats and species, marine protected areas, managing human activities to reduce their damaging impacts, and how marine ecosystems support our wellbeing.

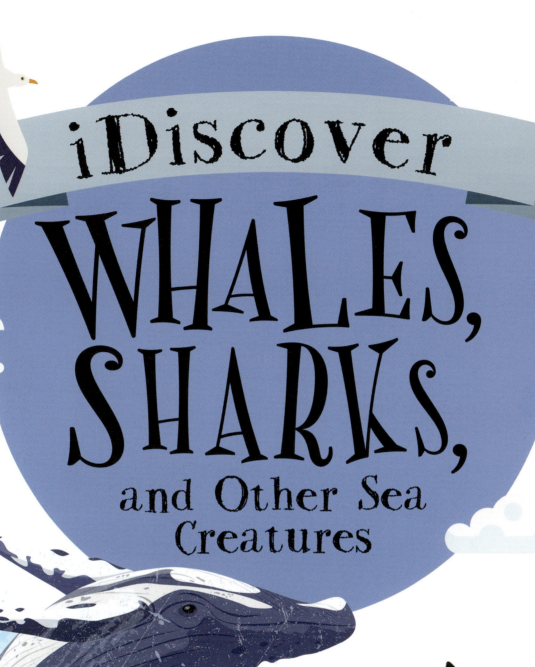

iDiscover

WHALES, SHARKS, and Other Sea Creatures

Written and Illustrated by
Carolyn Scrace

Consultant
Dr. Olivia Langmead

BOOK HOUSE
a SALARIYA imprint

Contents

- 6   What Lives In The Sea?
- 7   What Are Plankton?
- 8   Do Whales Have Teeth?
- 10   Can Whales Speak?
- 12   What Is A Shark?
- 13   Which Shark Is The Largest?
- 14   How Do Fish Breathe?
- 16   Are Dolphins Fish?
- 18   How Many Arms Does An Octopus Have?

20 How Big Are Squid?
21 What Are Jellyfish?
22 What Is A Coral Reef?
24 What Lives On The Seabed?
26 Do Turtles Swim Far?
28 What Lives Under The Ice?
30 Did You Know?
31 Glossary
32 Index

What Lives In The Sea?

The sea is vast—it covers about three-quarters of the Earth's surface. From shallow coastal waters to great ocean depths, the sea is home to a wide range of different plants and animals. Polar seas are cold, tropical seas are warm, and some inland seas are very salty.

The fish, whales, seals, and turtles that live in the sea are called vertebrates (animals with backbones). Those without a backbone like crabs, lobsters, jellyfish, squid, octopuses, sea urchins, starfish, and coral are called **invertebrates**.

What Are Plankton?

Plankton are very tiny plants and animals that drift in the sea's tides and currents. Flying fish, sardines, whale sharks, and huge filter-feeding whales eat plankton.

All living things need food to survive. Some animals eat plants, and they, in turn, may be eaten by other animals—this is called a **food chain.** The food chain starts with sea plants, seaweeds, and plankton that make their own food from sunlight.

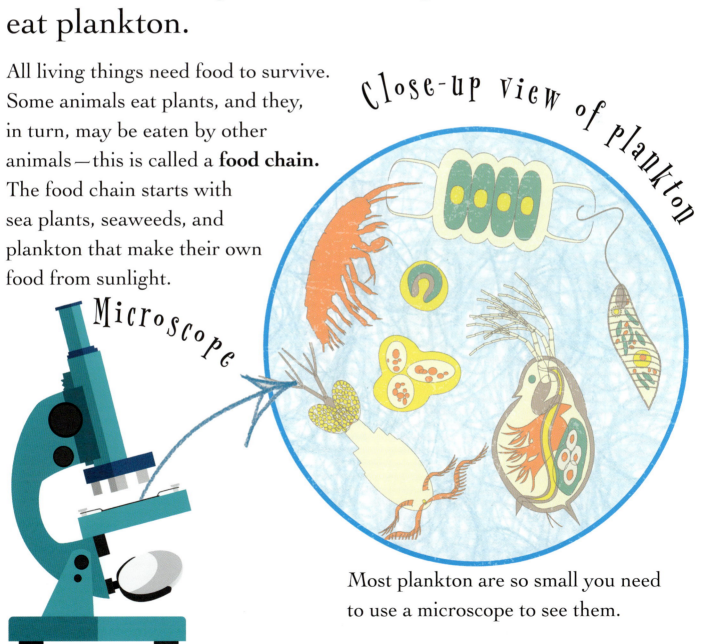

Most plankton are so small you need to use a microscope to see them.

7

Do Whales Have Teeth?

Some whales have teeth but baleen whales are **filter-feeders**. Instead, they have **baleen plates** with lots of comb-like bristles to trap food. Blue whales catch small, shrimp-like plankton called **krill** in their baleen.

A blue whale is the biggest animal in the world. It is about 100 feet (30 meters) long. That is as long as three buses parked in a row.

Blue whale

Ventral pleats

That's Heavy
A whale's tongue can weigh as much as an elephant!

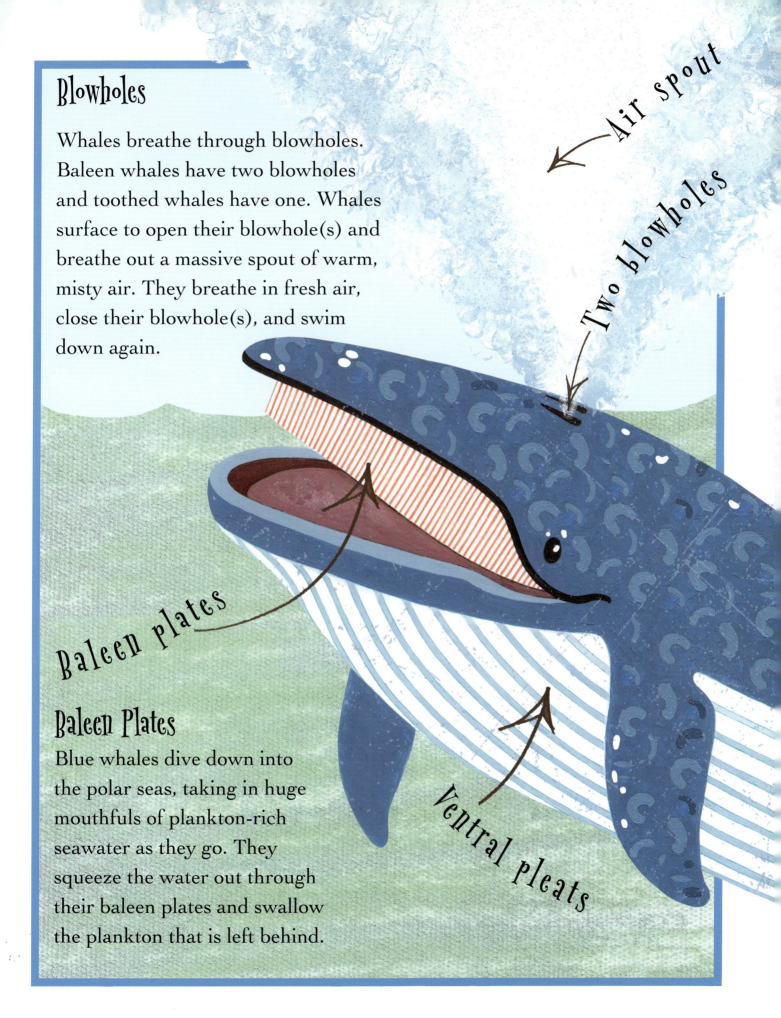

Blowholes

Whales breathe through blowholes. Baleen whales have two blowholes and toothed whales have one. Whales surface to open their blowhole(s) and breathe out a massive spout of warm, misty air. They breathe in fresh air, close their blowhole(s), and swim down again.

Baleen Plates

Blue whales dive down into the polar seas, taking in huge mouthfuls of plankton-rich seawater as they go. They squeeze the water out through their baleen plates and swallow the plankton that is left behind.

Humpback whale

Humpback Whale

Humpback whales jump high out of the water, slapping the surface with their tails as they come down. The slapping noise carries deep below the surface and may be a way of communicating.

Can Whales Speak?

Whales travel in groups called pods. They make various noises to communicate with each other. The three main types of sounds made by whales are clicks, whistles, and pulsed calls that sound like squeaks.

Narwhal

Narwhals live in Arctic waters near Canada and Greenland. They have one really long tooth that looks like a horn or tusk. They use it to detect changes in water temperature, and for hunting fish.

Tooth

Narwhal

Sperm Whale

The sperm whale is the biggest toothed whale. It has the largest brain of any known animal, weighing about 18 pounds (8 kilograms).

Sperm whale

Click Click

Gray Whale

Gray whales swim to the bottom of the sea and turn on their side to scoop up mud and sand from the seabed. Their baleen plates filter out tiny worms and shrimp to eat.

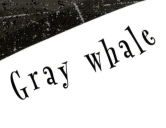

Gray whale

Great White Shark

The great white shark is the largest predatory fish in the sea. It has up to seven rows of sharp, pointed teeth—a never-ending supply! When a shark loses a tooth, another tooth takes its place.

Great white shark

Seal

Great white sharks take prey by surprise. They swim below it and, with a burst of speed, launch their attack. They often leap out of the water as they make their catch.

What Is A Shark?

Sharks are **cold-blooded** sea creatures. They have muscular, streamlined bodies and breathe with **gills**. They are very intelligent animals with large brains and good memories.

Whale shark

Which Shark Is The Largest?

The largest shark is the whale shark. It can grow up to 40 feet (12 meters) long. Instead of being fierce predators like most sharks, these huge creatures eat plankton and tiny fish.

How Do Fish Breathe?

Fish can breathe because their gills pick up oxygen from the water. Most fish are streamlined and have fins to help them balance and steer. Some fish live by themselves, while others live in huge shoals.

Dorsal fin

Swordfish

Gills

Pelvic fins

Swordfish

Swordfish are big fish with dorsal fins and long, sword-like bills. They mainly hunt at night using their sharp bills to slash at their prey.

Is An Eel A Fish?

Eels may look like snakes, but they are really fish. They have long, thin bodies and fins.

Moray eel

Flying fish

Can Fish Fly?

No, fish cannot fly. However flying fish look as if they are flying. Their big, wing-like fins help them to glide short distances above the surface of the water, to escape from predators.

Seahorse

A seahorse is a fish. It uses its long, thin snout to suck up tiny shrimp and fish food it finds. It wraps its long tail around seaweed or grasses to stop itself drifting away. Some seahorses change color to hide from predators.

Seahorse

Snout

Long tail

Deep-sea anglerfish

Lighted tip

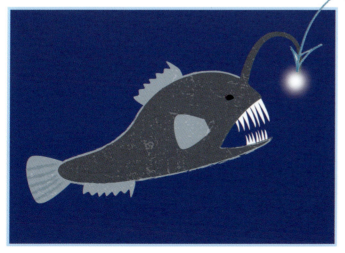

Can A Fish Make Light?

Many deep-sea fish make their own light. Above the female anglerfish's huge mouth is a light tipped rod to attract its prey.

Are Dolphins Fish?

No, dolphins are **mammals**. They live together in groups called pods. Dolphins are very intelligent. Each one develops its own signal of whistles and clicks so it can be identified underwater.

How High?
The Atlantic bottlenose dolphin can dive down to 984 feet (300 meters) and jump about 20 feet (6 meters) out of the water.

Dolphin

Whistle, click

Squid

Dolphins mainly eat fish and squid. They have about 100 teeth, which they use to grab their prey. They swallow their food whole without chewing it.

Killer Whale

Despite its name, a killer whale is not a whale! It is the largest of the dolphin family.

Killer whales on the hunt

Hunting

Killer whales hunt in pods and use **echolocation** to find prey. They make clicking sounds, then listen for echoes bouncing off fish, seals, and other animals. Once located, the whales encircle their prey, making it easier to attack.

Outgoing clicks

Incoming echoes

Killer whales have very good hearing. Finding prey by sound means that they don't need to see it and can hunt in total darkness.

How Many Arms Does An Octopus Have?

An octopus has eight arms which are covered in suckers. It uses its strong arms and suckers to grab and taste things.

Suckers

How Does An Octopus Hunt?

Most octopuses live in dens on the ocean floor and hunt mainly at night. They catch prey with their arms, then bite and kill them. Poisons soften the prey's flesh for the octopus to suck out.

When attacked, octopuses squirt blue-black ink to escape predators.

Octopus ink

An octopus can change color.

Octopus Swimming

An octopus swims by drawing water into its bag-like body and then squirting it out again. As the water squirts out, it pushes the octopus forwards.

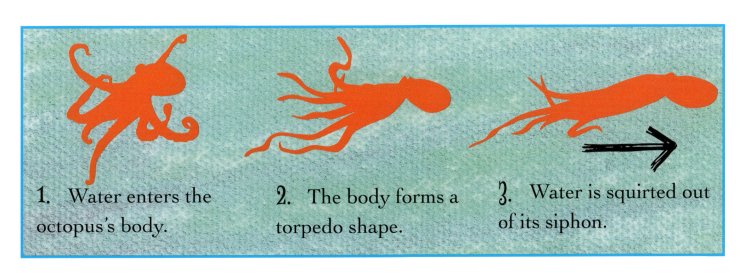

1. Water enters the octopus's body.
2. The body forms a torpedo shape.
3. Water is squirted out of its siphon.

How Big Are Squid?

A giant squid may grow up to 59 feet (17.9m) long. They have the largest eyes in the animal kingdom—about the size of dinner plates!

Giant squid

Squid and octopuses are called cephalopods, which means "head-foot." This is because their feet, or arms, are joined to their head.

What Do Squid Eat?

Squid and octopuses eat all kinds of sea creatures, from tiny shrimp, limpets, and worms, to lobsters and huge fish. Squid even eat other squid and octopuses.

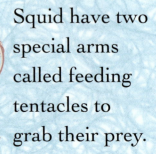

Squid

Squid have two special arms called feeding tentacles to grab their prey.

Sea nettle jellyfish

What Are Jellyfish?

Jellyfish have a smooth, bag-like body and most have stinging tentacles. A jellyfish uses its sting to paralyze its prey before it eats it.

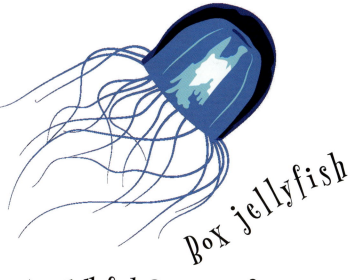

Box jellyfish

Are Jellyfish Dangerous?

Most jellyfish are harmless to humans, but the box jellyfish's venom can be deadly. Their sting is so painful that people have died of shock.

What Is A Coral Reef?

A coral reef is a stony ridge found under the sea. It is formed from the hard skeletons deposited by colonies of tiny animals, the coral polyps. Hundreds of types of fish and sea creatures feed on the coral or use it as a home. There are many different colored corals.

Soft coral

Bannerfish

Clownfish

Clownfish live within the sea anemone's poisonous tentacles to hide from predators. The clownfish keeps the anemone clean by eating **algae** and any food scraps on it.

Clownfish

Anemone

Giant clam

Black-tipped reef shark

Black-tipped Reef Shark
Black-tipped reef sharks produce live young and give birth to up to 10 "pups." Of over 400 different species of shark, nearly half lay eggs!

Masked butterfly fish

Moray eel

Parrotfish
Parrotfish eat the algae that grow on rocks and coral. They scrape it off with their hard, beak-like mouths.

Fan coral

Brain coral

Parrotfish

What Lives On The Seabed?

The seabed may be sandy, rocky, or covered with mud or gravel. Each seabed type has a community of different animals that lives there. Crabs, lobsters, prawns, starfish, and marine snails crawl along rocky reefs in search of food.

Crabs, Lobsters, and Prawns

Crabs, lobsters, and prawns all have a hard shell and two pairs of **antennae** or feelers. Crabs and lobsters have ten legs. Their front two legs have strong claws for gripping.

Hermit Crab

Unlike other crabs, hermit crabs don't have a hard outer shell. To protect their soft bodies they look for an empty shell to live in.

Starfish

Starfish are not fish, they are relatives of sea urchins. Their soft bodies are protected by a spiky shell. Most starfish have five arms but some species can have up to forty!

Prawns

Prawns have 5 pairs of swimming legs. If frightened, a prawn can shoot along backwards to hide under seaweed.

Seaweed

Prawn

Lobster

Lobsters live under or in between rocks. They have poor eyesight and use their sensitive antennae, legs, and feet to find food.

Do Turtles Swim Far?

Yes! Like many sea creatures, turtles make regular journeys at certain times of the year to find food or to breed. This is called migration. Turtles, penguins, and seals all migrate long distances from the sea to lay eggs or to give birth on land.

Leatherback turtle

Jellyfish

Leatherback Turtle
Leatherback turtles are the largest sea turtles. They have no teeth so their diet consists of soft-bodied animals like jellyfish. Leatherbacks make the longest migration of any turtle, up to 12,000 miles (19,000 kilometers).

Turtles Lay Eggs

Sea turtles lay their eggs on land. Many lose their special nesting grounds when hotels or houses are built on them.

The female green turtle drags herself up the beach at night. She uses her back flippers to dig a nest in the sand, then lays about 115 eggs.

The baby turtles all hatch at the same time. Once hatched, they follow the light of the Moon and stars to reach the sea.

What Lives Under The Ice?

At the north and south poles the sea is very cold and salty. The only plants found there are plant plankton, which is eaten by tiny animals called krill.

Emperor Penguins

Birds don't live in the sea, but many types of bird depend on the sea for food. Emperor penguins have one chick each year which they fiercely protect. They live and breed in large groups, mainly eating fish, squid, and krill.

Emperor penguins

Penguins are the best adapted of all the sea birds. They have flippers instead of wings and can swim and dive for food.

Seals

Seals have a layer of fat called **blubber** and thick waterproof fur, which allows them to survive in icy waters.

Beluga Whale

Beluga whales are one of the smallest species of whales. They have no fin on their back so they can swim under floating ice.

Ringed seals use the thick claws on their front flippers to make breathing holes in the ice.

A bearded seal can sleep in the water with its head at the surface so it can breathe.

Ringed seal

Bearded seal

Beluga whale

Walrus

Walruses use their snouts to dig for food on the muddy seabed. They use their long tusks to make holes in the polar ice so that they can find food. Males also use their tusks for fighting.

Walrus

Did You Know?

The clicking sounds made by a sperm whale are one of the loudest known sounds used by any animal to communicate.

Hammerhead sharks' eyes are on either side of their weirdly-shaped heads. Their eyes are so wide apart that they can see all around them—behind, in front, above, and below.

Some types of jellyfish are larger than a human and others are as small as a pinhead.

Adult walruses are huge. They grow to up to 11.5 feet (3.5 meters) long and weigh the same as a small car!

Sharks have very weak jaws for their size, but they can still bite through their prey because their teeth are so sharp.

Crabs wave or drum their pincers to communicate with each other.

If a starfish's arm gets damaged or eaten by a predator, another arm will grow back to replace it.

Before going to sleep at night, a parrotfish uses slime from inside its mouth to make a sleeping bag. The bag protects it from predators.

An octopus has three hearts, nine brains, and blue blood. It has one central brain and a mini brain in each of its eight arms.

Dolphins keep half their brain awake when they are sleeping. This enables them to breathe while asleep and to stay safe from predators.

A jellyfish has no ears, eyes, or nose, and no brain or heart! Its body is mostly made of water.

Thresher shark

Glossary

Hammerhead shark

A
algae a simple form of plant.
antennae a pair of long thin organs on the heads of crustaceans and some other animals.

B
baleen plates stiff, bristle-like plates that hang down from the upper jaws of baleen whales. Used to strain plankton from seawater.
blubber the thick layer of fat on whales, seals, and other sea mammals.

C
cold-blooded an animal that cannot control its own body temperature and relies on the surrounding air or water temperature.

E
echolocation how some animals locate an object by reflected sound.

F
filter-feeder an animal that filters tiny bits of food from water that passes through part of its body.
food chain how different kinds of animals are linked to each other because they each become the food supply of the next in the chain.

G
gills body parts that animals, like fish, use to breathe underwater.

I
invertebrate an animal without a backbone.

K
krill very small, shrimp-like animals that live in the sea.

M
mammal warm-blooded animals with hair or fur that usually give birth to live young.
migration the seasonal movement of animals from one area to another in search of food or to breed.

P
plankton tiny plants and animals that drift and float in the sea.

V
ventral pleats expand when a whale is feeding so that its stomach can hold huge amounts of food.
vertebrate an animal with a spine.

Index

A
algae 22–23, 31
anemone 22

B
baleen 8–9, 11, 31
blowhole 9

C
coral 6, 22–23
coral reef 22
crab 6, 24–25, 30

D
dolphins 16–17, 30

E
echolocation 17, 31

F
filter-feeding 7–8, 31
fins 14–15, 29
fish 6–7, 11–17, 20, 22–23, 28, 30–31
food chain 7, 31

G
gills 12, 14, 31

J
jellyfish 6, 21, 26, 30

K
krill 8, 28, 31

L
leatherback turtle 26
lobster 6, 20, 24–25

M
migration 26, 31
moray eel 14, 23

O
octopus 6, 18–20, 30

P
penguins 26, 28
plankton 7–9, 13, 28, 31
pods 10, 16–17
prawns 24–25

S
seahorse 15
seals 6, 12, 17, 26, 29, 31
sharks 7, 12–13, 23, 30–31
squid 6, 16, 20, 28
starfish 6, 24–25, 30
stinging tentacles 21
suckers 18

T
tentacles 20–22
toothed whale 9, 11
turtle 6, 26–27
tusk 11, 29

V
ventral pleats 8–9, 31

W
walrus 29–30
whales 6–11, 13, 17, 29–31